McBroom's Ghost

Library of Congress Cataloging-in-Publication Data

Fleischman, Sid, 1920-
   McBroom's ghost / by Sid Fleischman ; illustrated by Amy Wummer.
      p.   cm. — (The adventures of McBroom)
   Summary: The McBroom family is plagued by a mysterious ghost that visits their amazing
one-acre farm after every prolonged freezing spell.
   [1. Ghosts—Fiction. 2. Farms—Fiction. 3. Humorous stories. 4. Tall tales.] I. Wummer, Amy, ill.
II. Title. III. Series: Fleischman, Sid, 1920- Adventures of McBroom.
PZ7.F5992Mag 1998
[Fic]—dc21   98-26695
                                                                                                          CIP
ISBN 0-8431-7948-1 (pbk.) A B C D E F G H I J   AC

ISBN 0-8431-7899-X (GB)   A B C D E F G H I J

McBroom's Ghost

By
Sid Fleischman

Illustrated by
Amy Wummer

PSS!
PRICE STERN SLOAN

Ghosts? Mercy, yes—I can tell you a thing or three about ghosts. As sure as my name's Josh McBroom a haunt came lurking about our wonderful one-acre farm.

I don't know when that confounded dry-bones first moved in with us, but I suspicion it was last winter. An *uncommon* cold winter it was, too, though not so cold that an honest man would tell fibs about it. Still, you had to be careful when you lit a match. The flame would freeze and you had to wait for a thaw to blow it out.

Some old-timers declared that was just
a middling cold winter out here on the
prairie. Nothing for the record books.
Still, we did lose our rooster, Sillibub.

He jumped on the woodpile, opened
his beak to crow the break of day,
and the poor thing quick-froze as
stiff as glass.

The way I reckoned it, that ghost was whisking about and got icebound on our farm.

The young'uns were the first to discover the pesky creature. A March thaw had come along and they had gone outside to play. I was bundled up in bed with the laryngitis—hadn't been able to speak above a whisper for three days. I passed the time listening to John Philip Sousa's band on our talking machine. My, those piccolos did sound pretty!

Suddenly the young'uns were back and they appeared kind of strange in the eyes.

"Pa," said our youngest boy, Larry. "Pa, do roosters ever turn into ghosts?"

I tried to clear my throat. "Never heard of such a thing," I croaked.

"But we just this minute heard old Sillibub *crow*," said our oldest girl, Jill.

"Impossible, my lambs," I whispered, and they went out to frolic in the sun again.

I cranked up the talking machine, and once more Mr. Sousa's band came marching and trilling out of the morning-glory horn. Suddenly the young'uns were back—all eleven of them.

"We heard it again," said Will.

"*Cock-a-doodle-do!*" Little Clarinda crowed. "Plain as day, Pa. Out by the woodpile."

I shook my head. "Must be Mr. Sousa's piccolos you're hearing," I said hoarsely, and they went out to play again.

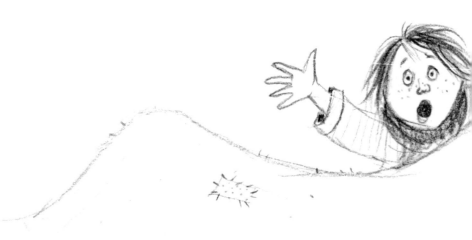

I cranked up the machine and before
I knew it the young'uns came flocking
back in.

"Yes, Pa?" Will said.

"Yes, Pa?" Jill said.

"You called, Pa?" Hester said.

I lifted the needle off the record and gazed at them. "Called?" I croaked. Then I laughed hoarsely. "Why, you scamps know I can't raise my voice above a whisper. Aren't you full of mischief today!"

"But we *heard* you, Pa," Chester said.

"'Will*jill*hester*chester*peter*polly*tim*tom*mary*larry*andlittle*clarinda*!'" Polly said. "It was your very own voice, Pa. And plain as day."

Well, after that they wouldn't go back out to play. They were certain some scaresome thing was roving about. Sure enough, the next morning we were awakened at dawn by the crowing of a rooster. It did sound like old Sillibub. But I said, "Heck Jones must have got himself a rooster. That's what we hear."

"But Heck Jones doesn't keep chickens," my dear wife Melissa reminded me. "You know he's raising hogs, Pa. The meanest, wildest hogs I ever saw. I do believe he hopes they'll root up our farm and drive us out."

Heck Jones was our neighbor, and an almighty torment to us. He was tall and scrawny and just as mean and ornery as those Arkansas razorback hogs of his. He'd tried more than once to get our rich one-acre farm for himself.

It wouldn't surprise me if he was
making those queer noises himself. Well,
if he thought he could scare us off our
property he was mistaken!

By the time I got over the laryngitis the young'uns were afraid to leave the house. They just stared out the windows. Something was out there. They were certain of it.

So I bundled up and marched outside to look for Heck Jones's footprints in the mud. Well, I had hardly got as far as the woodpile when a voice came ripping out of the still air.

"Will*jill*hester*chester*peter*polly*tim*tom*mary*larry*andlittle*clarinda*!"

That voice sounded *exactly* like my own. I spun about.

But there wasn't a soul to be seen.

I don't mind admitting that my hair shot up on end. It knocked my hat off.

There wasn't a footprint to be seen, either.

"Do you think the farm is haunted?"
Larry asked at supper.

"No," I answered firmly. "Haunts
clank chains and moan like the wind and
rap at doors."

Just then there came a rap at the door.
The young'uns all shot looks at me—
Mama, too.

Well, I got up and opened the door
and there was no one there.

That's when I had to admit there
was a dry-bones dodging about our
property. And mercy, what a sly,
prankster creature it was! When that
ghost wasn't mimicking old Sillibub, it
was mimicking me.

Well, we didn't sleep very well after that. Some nights I didn't sleep at all. I kept a sharp eye out for that haunt, but it never would show itself.

Finally, Mama and the young'uns began to talk about giving up the farm. Then we had another freeze, and for three solid weeks that spirit didn't make a sound. We reckoned it had moved away.

We breathed easier, I can tell you! There was no more talk of leaving the farm. The young'uns passed the time leafing through the mail-order catalogue, and we all listened to the talking machine.

"Pa, we'd dearly love to have a dog,"
Jill said one day.

"You won't find dogs in the mail-order
catalogue, my lambs," I said.

"We know, Pa," said Chester. "But can't
we have a dog? A big, shaggy
farm dog?"

I shook my head sadly. A dog would be the ruination of our amazing rich one-acre farm. There was nothing that wouldn't grow in that remarkable soil of ours—and quicker'n scat. I thought back to the summer day Little Clarinda had lost a baby tooth. By time we found it, that tooth had grown so large we had to put up a block and tackle to extract it.

"No," I said. "Dogs dig holes and bury bones. Those bones would grow the size of buried logs. I'm sorry, my lambs."

The icicles began to melt in the spring thaw—and there came another knock at the door.

The haunt was back!

That night the young'uns slept huddled together all in one bed. Didn't I pace the floor, though! That door-rapping, rooster-crowing, me-mimicking dry-bones would drive us off our farm. Unless I drove it off first.

Early the next morning I trudged through the mud to town. Everyone said that the Widow Witherbee was a ghost seer.

I called on her first thing. She was a spry little cricket of a lady who bought and sold hand-me-down clothes. But tarnation! Her eyesight was failing and she said she couldn't spy out ghosts anymore.

"What am I to do?" I asked, as a litter of mongrel pups nipped at my ankles.

"Simple," the Widow Witherbee said. "Burn a pile of old shoes. Never fails to drive ghosts away."

Well, that sounded like twaddle to me, but I was desperate. She went poking through rags and old clothes, and I bought all the worn-out, hand-me-down shoes she could find.

"You'll also need a dog," she said.

My eyebrows shot up. "A dog?"

"Certainly," she said. "Certainly. How are you going to know if you ran off that haunt without a dog? Hounds can see ghosts. Mongrels are best. When their ears stand up and they freeze and point like a bird dog—you know they're staring straight at a ghost. Then you have to burn more shoes."

So I bought one of her flop-eared pups and started back for the farm, carrying a bushel basket of old shoes.

As I approached the house I could see the young'uns' faces at the windows. Piccolos were trilling merrily in the air.

But dash it all! When I opened the door I saw that no one had a record on the talking machine.

"Confound that haunt!" I exploded. "Now it's imitating John Philip Sousa's entire marching band!"

Of course, the young'uns couldn't believe I had brought home a dog. It was the first time all winter long I saw smiles on their faces. Didn't they gather around him, though! They promised to keep close watch so that he wouldn't bury any bones.

I didn't lose any time burning that bushel of old shoes. Mercy, what an infernal strong smell! I could imagine that dry-bones holding its nose and rattling away, never to return.

Every day after that we walked the pup around the farm, and never once did he raise his flop ears and point.

"By ginger!" I exclaimed finally. "The old shoes did it. That haunt is gone!"

By that time the young'uns had decided
on a name for the pup. They called him
Zip. He grew up to be the handiest farm
dog I ever saw.

That rich soil of ours was rarin' to go,
and we started our spring planting—
raised a crop of tomatoes and two crops
of carrots the first day. In no time at all the
young'uns taught Zip to dig a furrow.
Straight as a beeline, too!

But our troubles weren't over with that ghost chased off. One burning hot morning we planted the farm in corn. The stalks came busting up through the ground, leafing out and dangling with ears. I tell you, Heck Jones's hogs acted as if we had rung the dinner bell. Mercy! They came roaring down on us in a snorting, squealing, thundering herd.

"Will*jill*hester*chester*peter*polly*tim*tom*mary*larry*andlittle*clarinda*!" I shouted. "And Zip! Run for your lives!"

Those hungry, half-wild razorback hogs broke down the stalks and gorged themselves on sweet ears of corn. Then they rooted up the farm looking for leftover carrots.

Well, those razorbacks finally trotted home with their stomachs scraping the ground, and I followed along behind.

"Heck Jones," I said. He was standing in a cloud of flies and eating a shoofly pie. It was mostly made of molasses and brown sugar, which attracted the flies and kept a body busy shooing them off. "Heck Jones, it appears to me you've been starving your hogs."

"Bless my soul, they don't look starved to me," he chuckled, shooing flies off his shoofly pie. "See for yourself, neighbor."

"Heck Jones," I said stoutly. "If you aim to raise hogs, I'd advise you to grow your own hog feed."

"No need for that, neighbor," he laughed. "There's plenty of feed about, and razorbacks can fend for themselves. Of course, if you hanker to give up farming, I might make an offer for that patch of ground you're working."

"Heck Jones," I said for the last time. I could hardly see him for the cloud of flies. "You're mistaken if you think you and your razorbacks can drive us off, sir. Either pen up those hogs, or I'll have the law on you!"

"There's no law says I've got to pen my hogs," he said, finishing off the pie and a few flies in the bargain. "Anyway, neighbor, no pen would hold the rascals."

Well, I'll admit he was right about that. We fenced our farm, but those infernal hogs busted through it and scattered the pieces like a cyclone. We strung barbed wire. It only stopped them long enough to scratch their backs. Barbed wire was a *comfort* to those razorbacks.

I tell you, we battled those hogs all spring and summer. We planted a crop of prickly pear cactus, but not even that kept the herd out. They ate the pears and picked their teeth with the prickly spines.

All the while, Heck Jones stood on the brow of the hill eating shoofly pies and going, "Hee-*haw!* Hee-*haw!*" His hogs grew fatter and fatter. I tell you, we were lucky to save enough garden sass for our own table.

Another growing season like that and we'd be ruined!

3

Then summer came to an end, and
we knew we were in for more than an
uncommon cold winter. It was going
to be a *dreadful* cold winter. There
were signs.

I remember that the boys had gone
fishing in late October and brought home
a catfish. *That catfish had grown a coat of
winter fur.*

That wasn't all. After the first fall of
snow, the young'uns built a snowman.

The next morning it was gone. We found out later that snowman had gone *south* for the winter.

Well, it turned out to be the Winter of the Big Freeze. I don't intend to stray from the facts, but I distinctly remember one day Polly dropped her comb on the floor, and when she picked it up the teeth were chattering.

As things turned out, that was just a middling cold day in the Winter of the Big Freeze. The temperature kept dropping, and I must admit some downright *unusual* things began to happen.

For one thing, smoke took to freezing in the chimney. I had to blast it out with a shotgun three times a day. And we couldn't sit down to a bowl of Mama's hot soup before a crust of ice formed on top. The girls used to set the table with a knife, a fork, a spoon—and an ice pick.

Well, the temperature kept dropping, but we didn't complain. At least there was no ghost lurking about, and Heck Jones's hogs stayed home, and the young'uns had the dog to play with. I kept cranking the talking machine.

Then the *big* freeze set in. Red barns for miles around turned blue with the cold. There's many an eyewitness to that! One day the temperature fell so low that sunlight froze on the ground.

Now, I disbelieved that myself. So I scooped up a chunk in a frying pan and brought it inside. Sure enough, I was able to read to the young'uns that night by the glow of that frozen chunk of winter sun.

Of course, we had our share of
wolves about. Many a night, through
the windows, we could see great packs
of them trying their best to howl. I
suspicioned laryngitis. Those wolves
couldn't make a sound. It was pitiful.

4

Well, spring thaw came at last. I remember stepping outside and the first thing I heard was a voice.

"Hee-*haw!*"

"What mischief are you up to now, Heck Jones!" I answered back.

But as I looked about me, I saw there wasn't another soul on the farm.

Then I knew. My hair rose, knocking my hat to the ground again. That door-rapping, rooster-crowing, me-mimicking, hee-*hawing* ghost was back!

"Zip!" I shouted, and we went tracking all over the farm. Voices popped up behind us and in front of us and around the woodpile.

But that dog of ours never once lifted his flop ears.

"Confound it!" I grumbled to Mama and the young'uns. "Zip can't see ghosts at all!"

The poor mongrel knew I was dreadful disappointed in him. He lit out through my legs and dug a straight furrow in the farm quick as I ever saw.

When that didn't bring a smile to my face, he zipped over to the corn bin and took a cob in his mouth. He'd watched us plant many a time. He ran back up the furrow, shelling the corn with his teeth and planting the kernels with a poke of his nose.

"Maybe Zip can't see ghosts," Will said. "But he's a powerful smart farm dog, Pa. Can't we still keep him?"

I didn't have a moment to answer. As the corn stalks shot up, Heck Jones appeared eating a shoofly pie on the rim of the hill. At the same instant, his razor-back hogs came thundering toward us— and that infernal haunt began trilling like a piccolo.

"Run for your lives!" I shouted.
We all ran but Zip. The corn was
ripening fast and he meant to *harvest* it.

I started back out the door to snatch
him up, but suddenly that prankish
ghost changed its tune. It began
howling like a pack of hungry wolves.

I stood my ground, scratching my
head. Sounds were breaking out
everywhere in the air. As if howling and
yipping like an entire pack of wolves
wasn't enough, that haunt joined in with
Mr. Sousa's entire marching band. I must
admit, it had those piccolos down perfect.

You never heard such a howling! And
didn't those hogs stop in their tracks! I
tell you they near jumped out of their
skins. That ghost kept yipping and
howling from every quarter. Heck Jones
didn't have a chance to *hee* and to *haw*.

Those razorbacks turned on their heels. They trampled him in the mud and kept running—though one of them did come back for the shoofly pie. My, they did run! I heard later they didn't stop until they arrived back in Arkansas, where they were mistaken for guinea pigs. They had run off that much weight.

"Yes, my lambs," I said to the young'uns. "Reckon we'll keep ol' Zip. Look at him harvest that corn!"

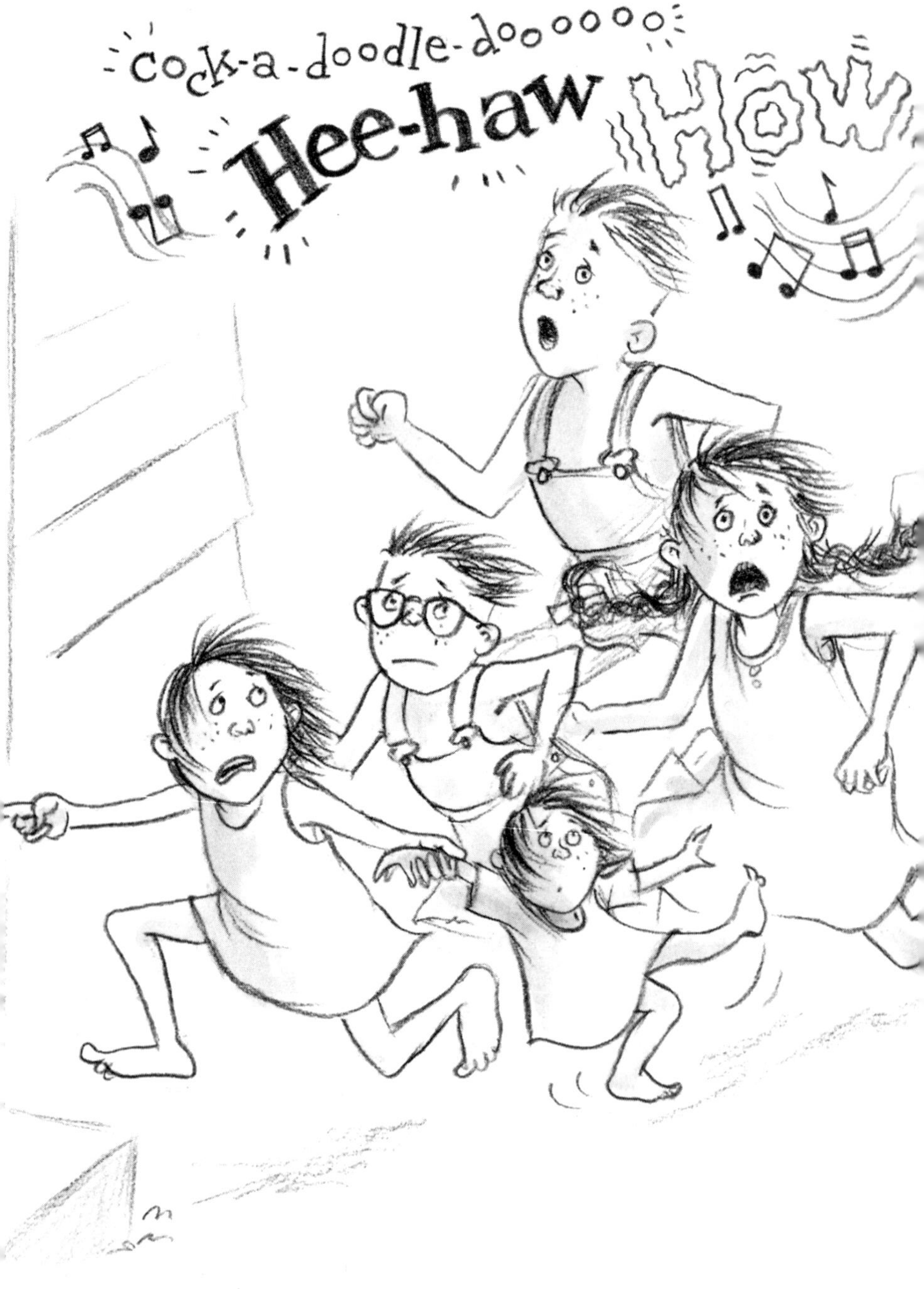

cock-a-doodle-doooooo
Hee-haw
HOW

Well, we'd got rid of Heck Jones's razorback hogs, but we still had that dry-bones cutting up. The young'uns remembered to be scared and streaked behind closed doors.

I kept scratching my head and suddenly I said to myself, "Why, there's no haunt around here. No wonder ol' Zip couldn't spy it out."

Glory be! It was clear to me now. There never *had* been a haunt lurking about! It was nothing but the weather playing pranks on us. No wonder we hadn't been able to hear wolves in the dead of winter. *The sounds had frozen.*

And now all those sounds were *thawing* out!

Well, it wasn't long before I coaxed the young'uns outside again, and soon they were enjoying the rappings at the door and the yips of wolves and shotgun blasts three times a day from the chimney top.

And didn't they laugh about Heck Jones's razorback hogs running from the howling and yipping of last winter's wolves!

Hee-haw!

Well, that's the truth about our prairie
winters and McBroom's ghost—as sure as
I'm a truthful man.